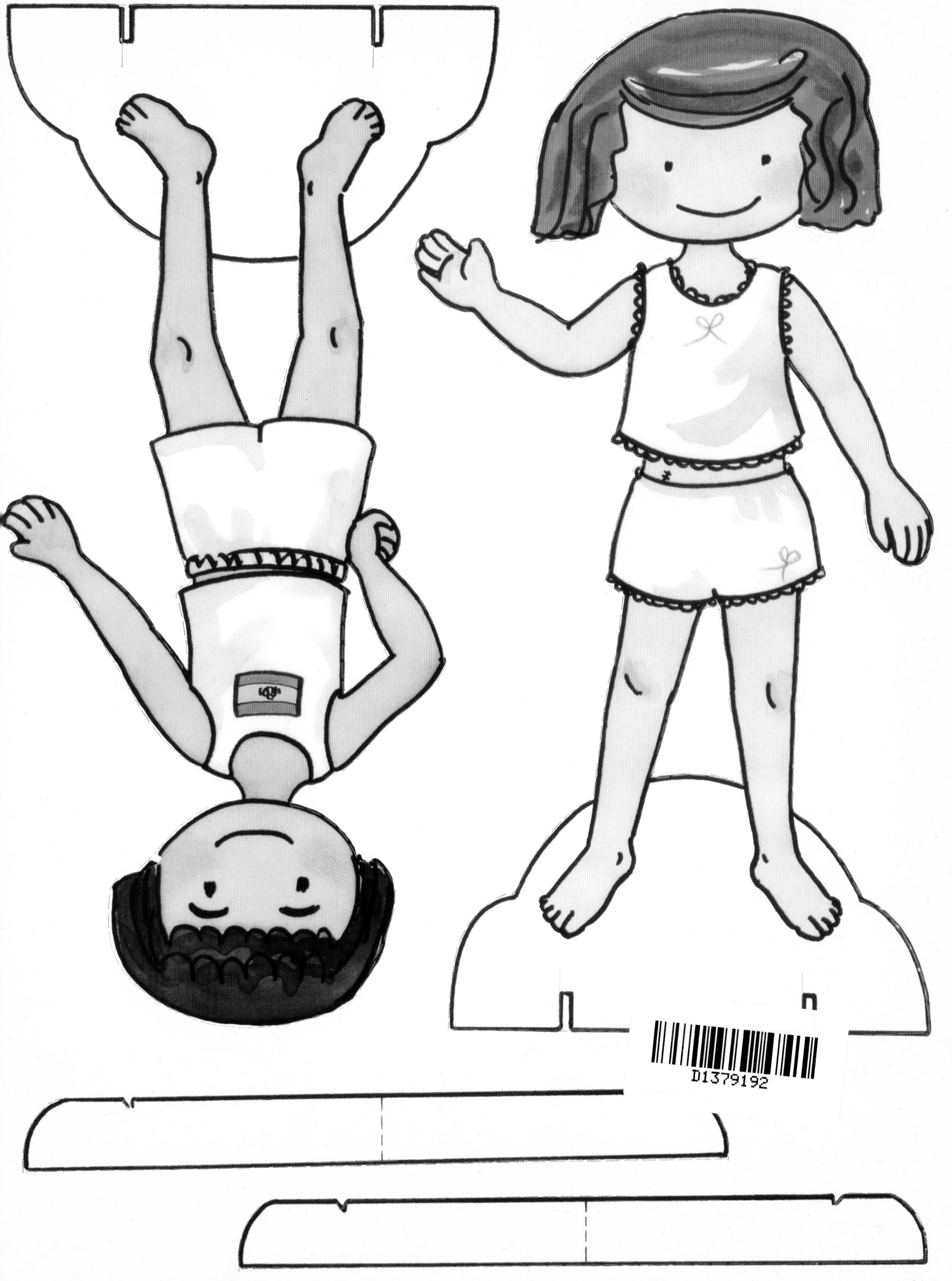

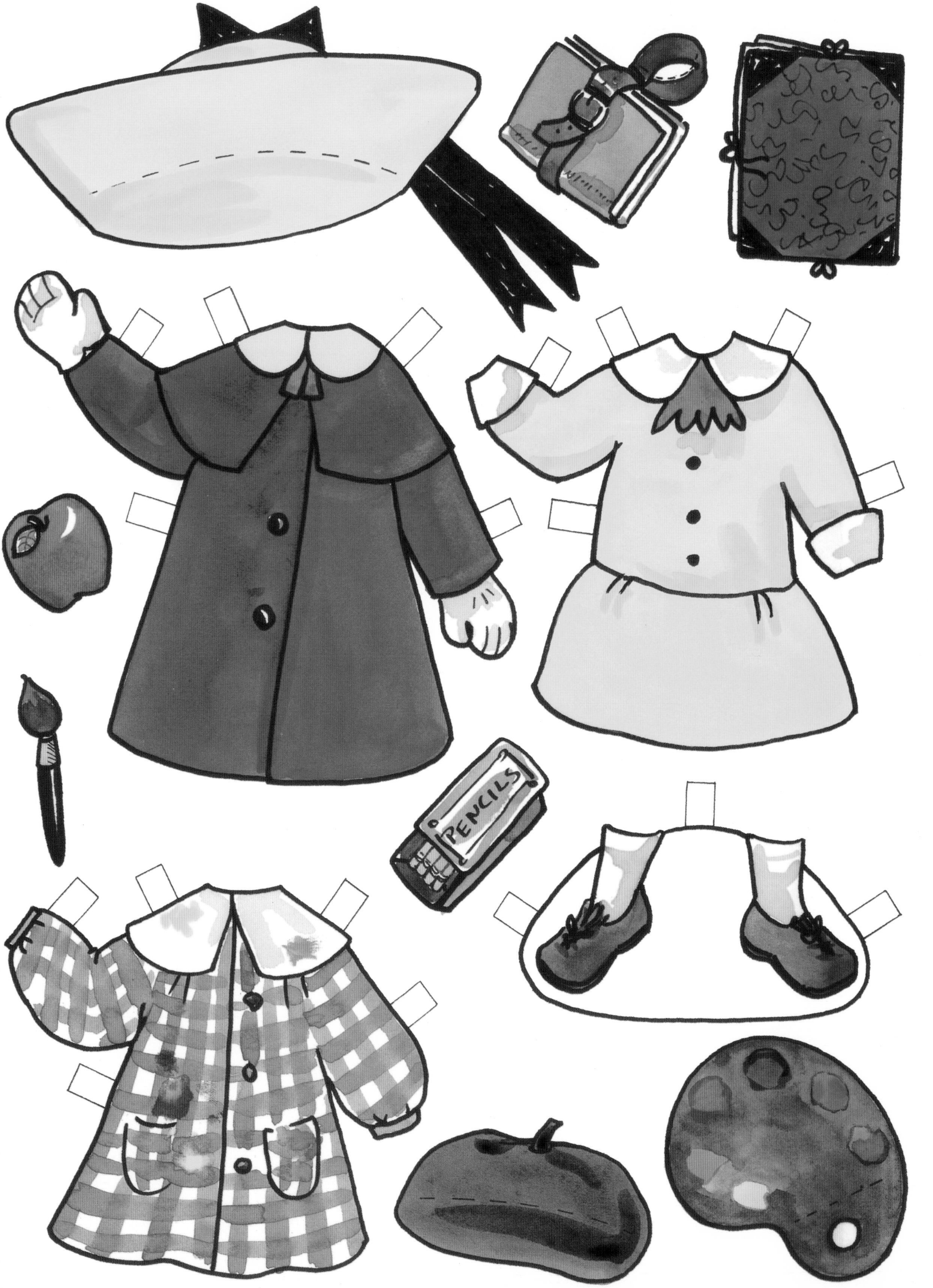
PENCILS

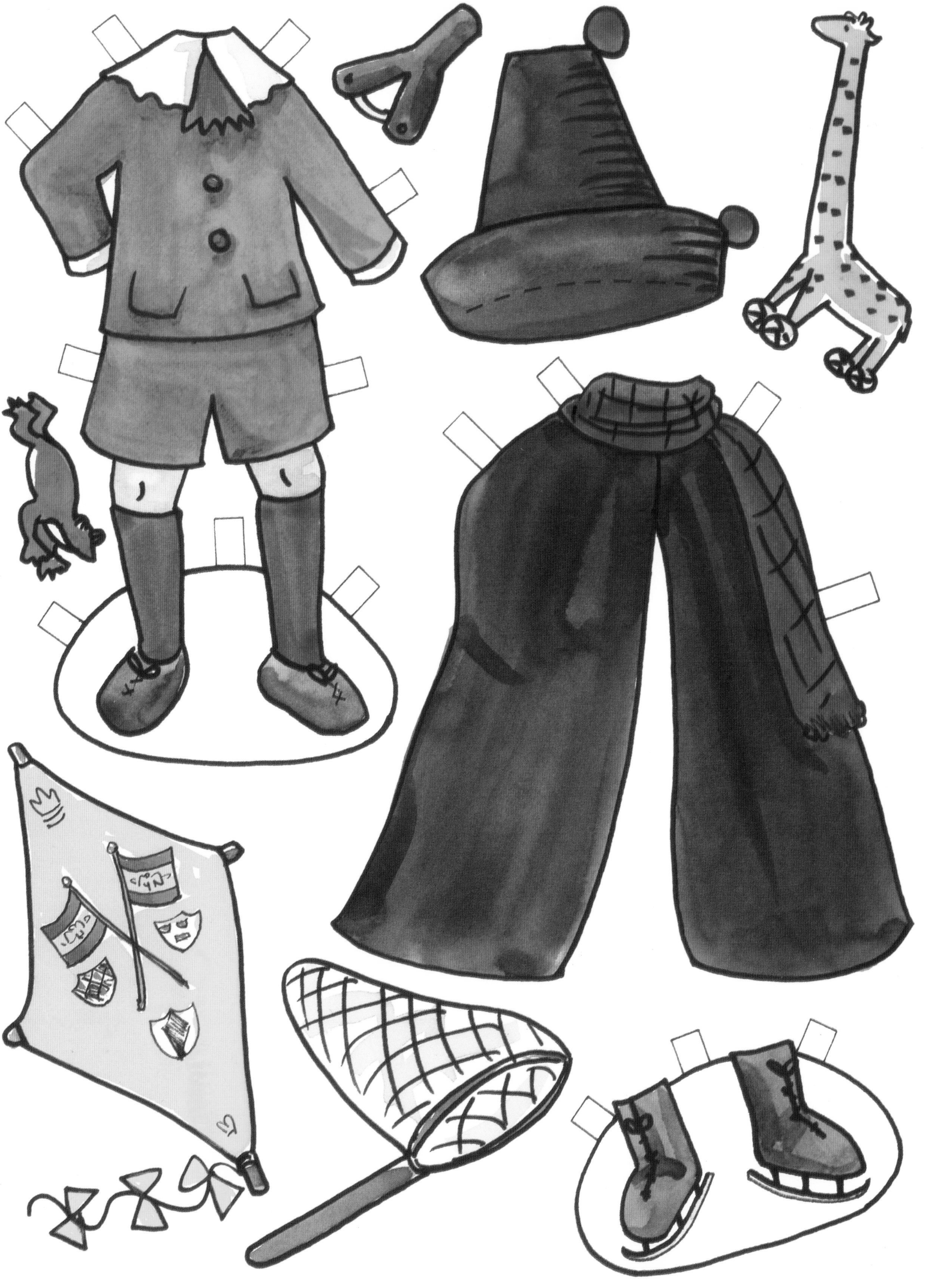

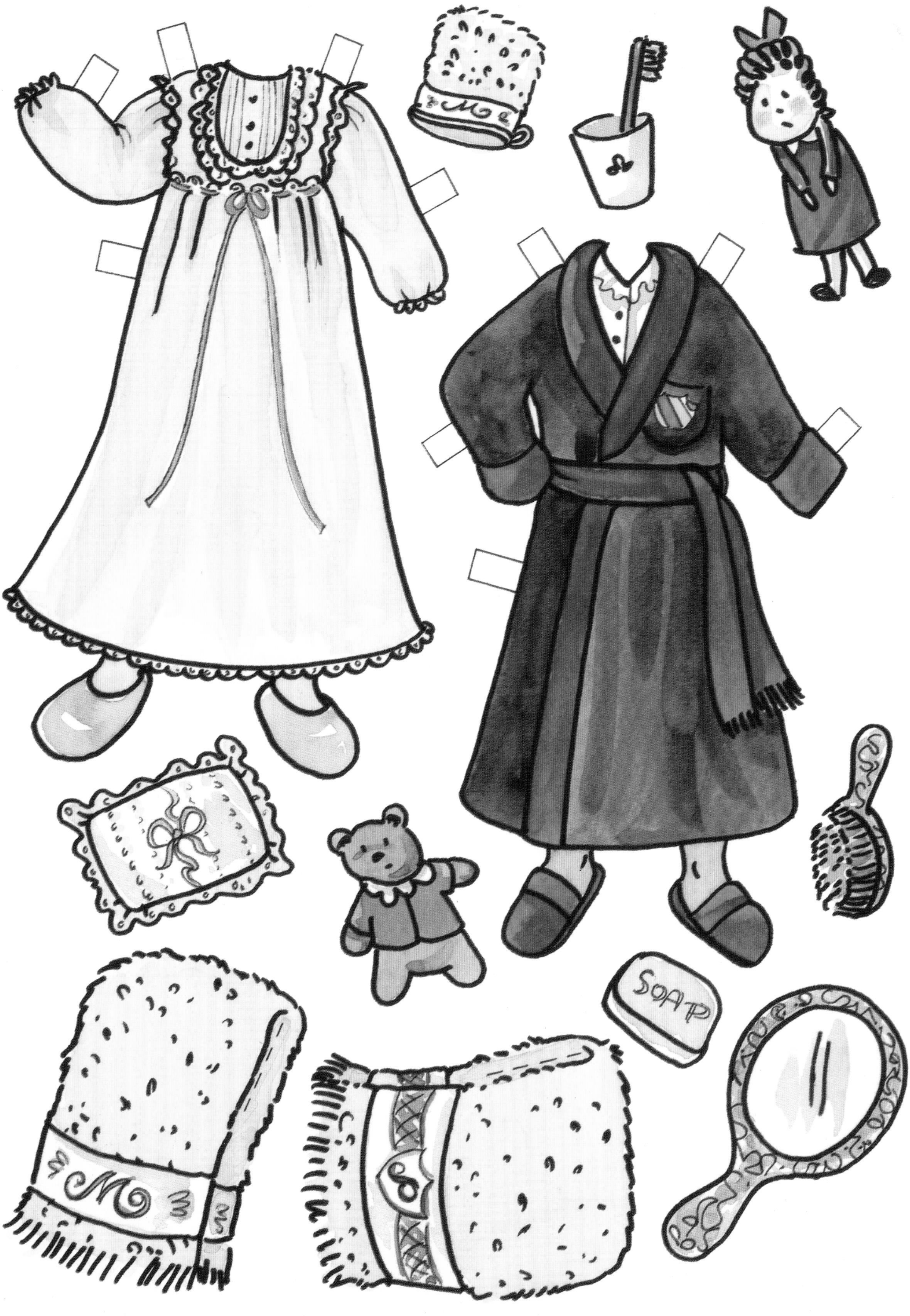
SOAP

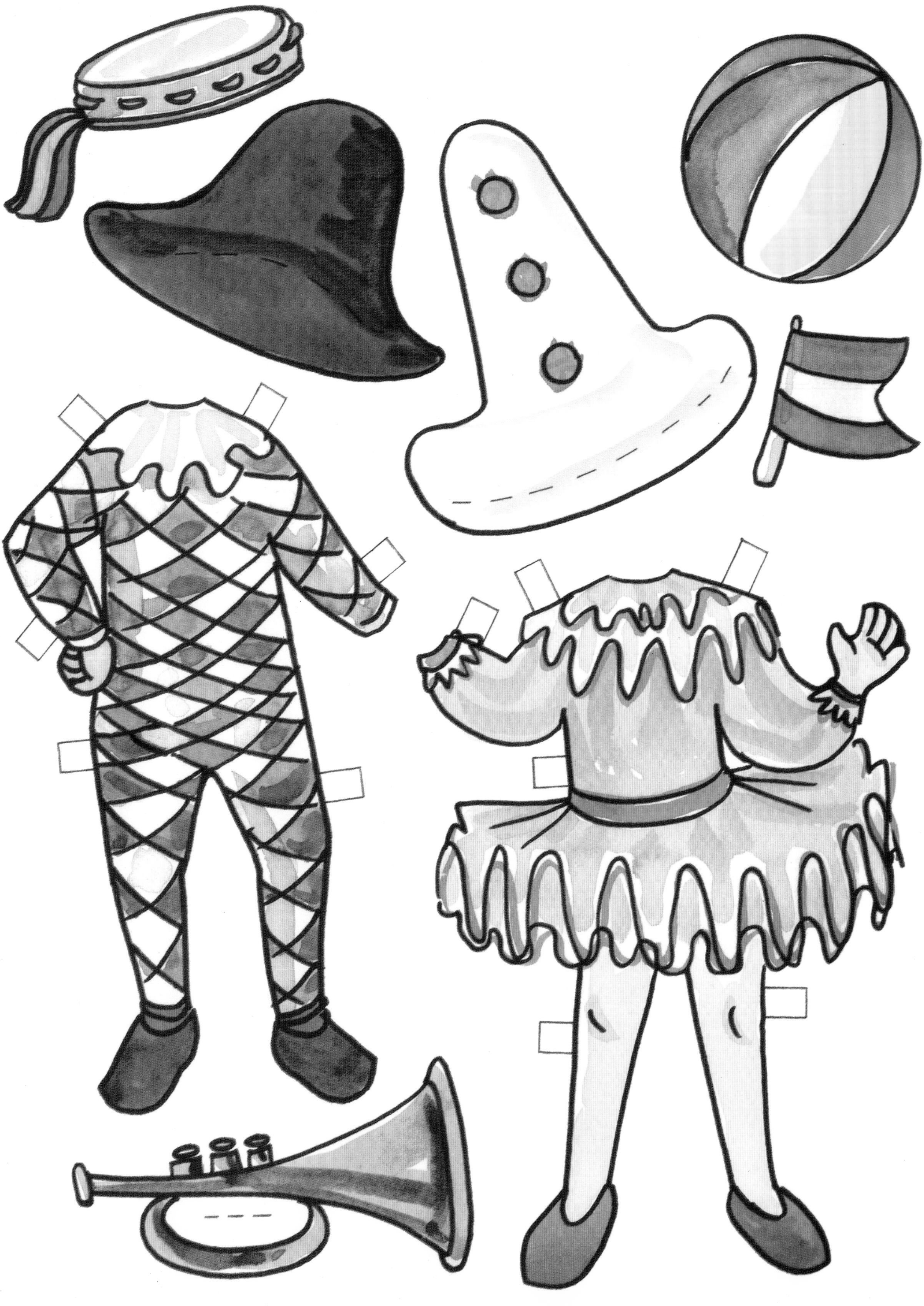

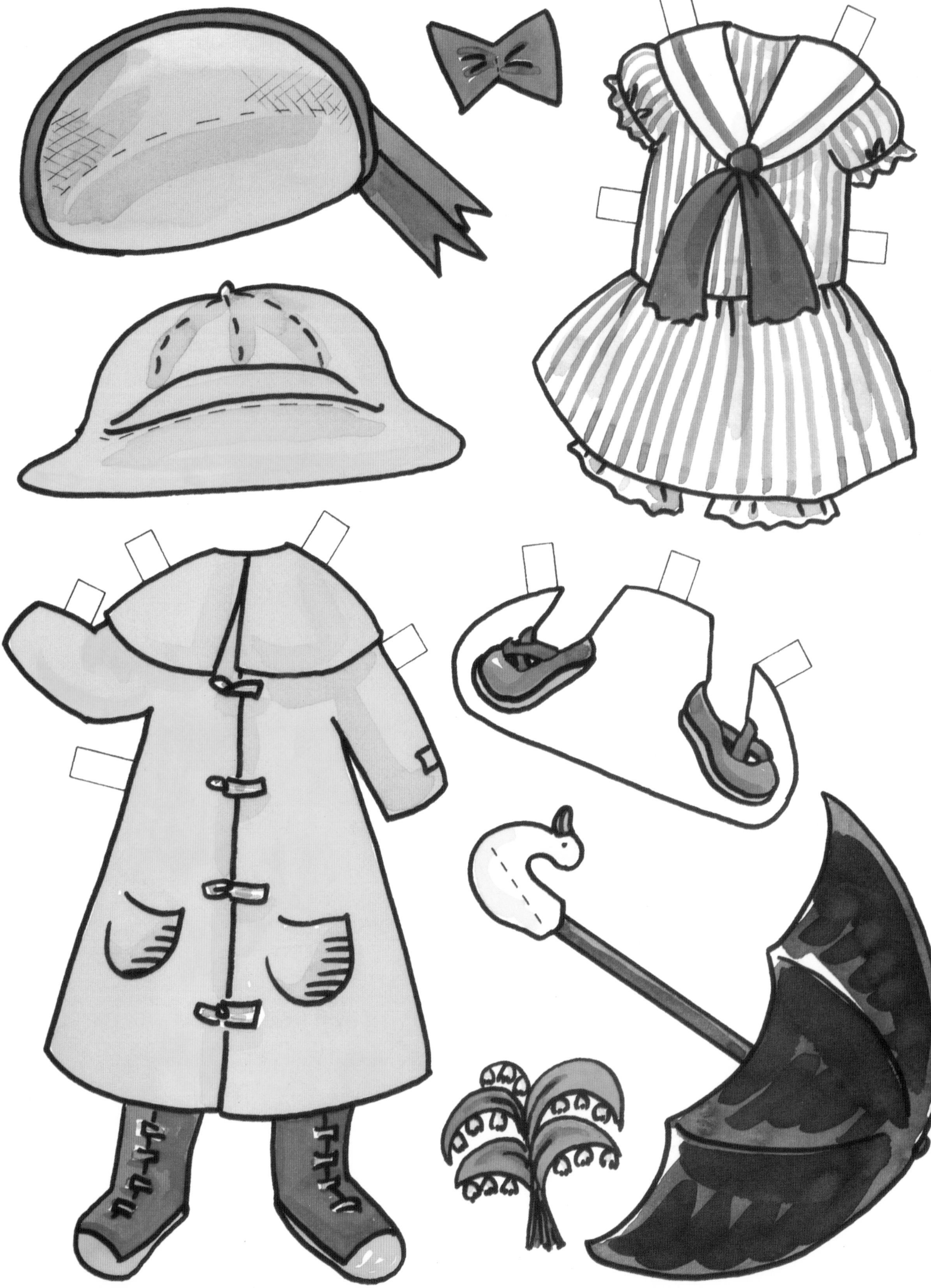

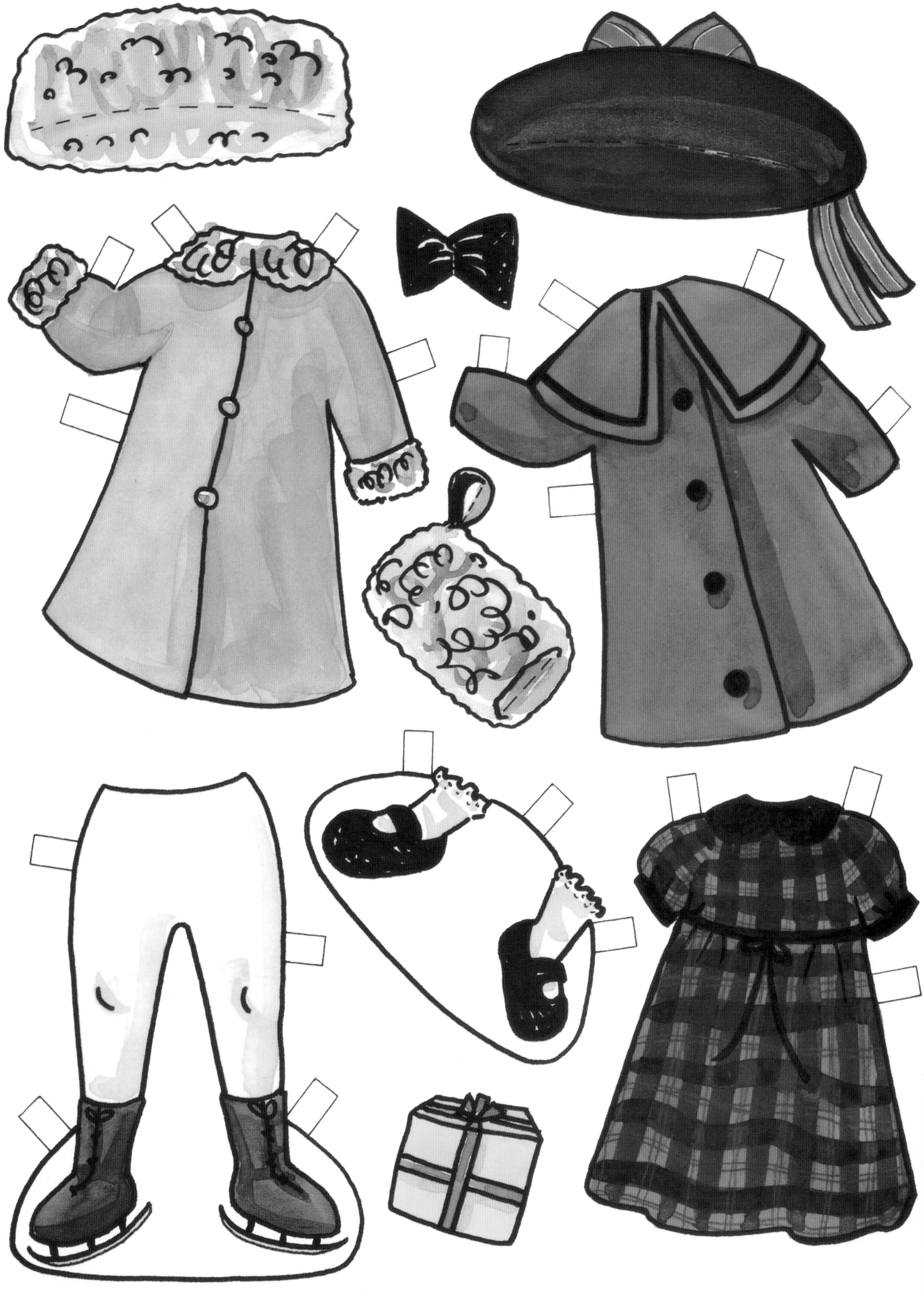

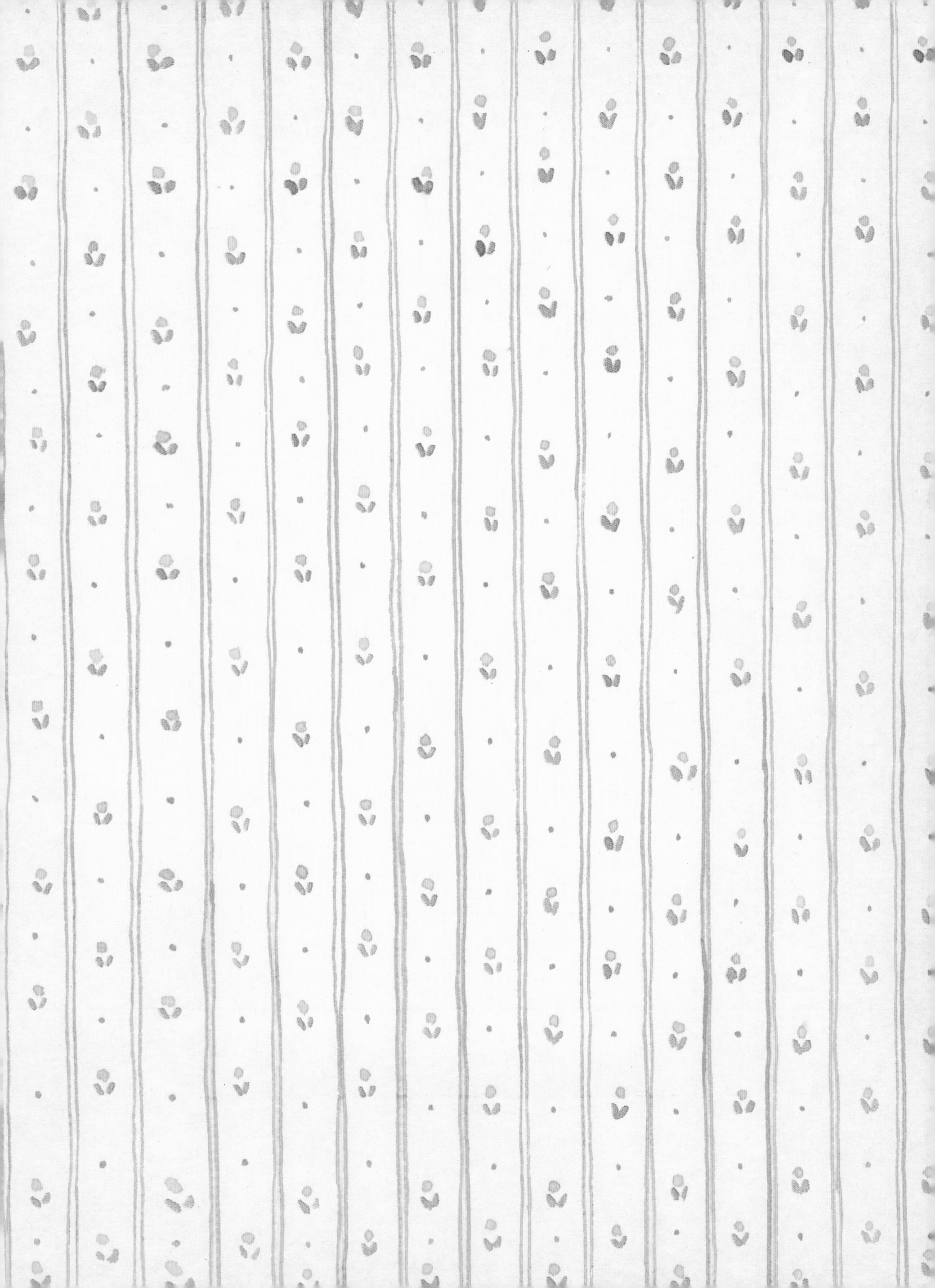

Armoire Back

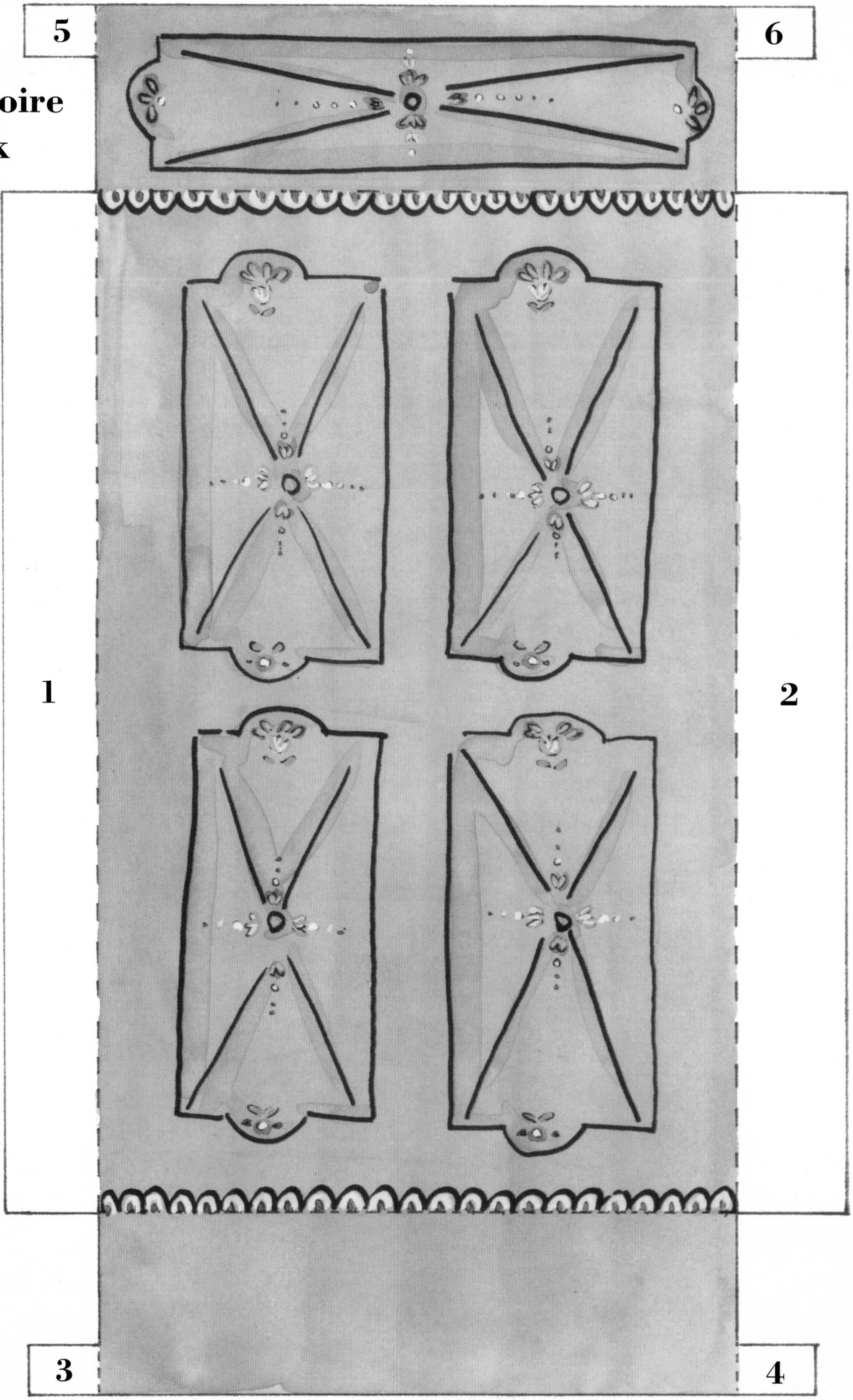